Just Like A Rainbow

Written by
LaJuana D Jackson

Illustrated by
Mariah Green

1

Copyright © 2020 Power of One LLC
Published by Power of One LLC
Belleville, MI 48112 USA
ISBN-13: 978-1-7351969-3-0

Illustrations by Mariah Green
Art Direction by Justin Perkins

First Printing: 2021

Dedication

I dedicate "Just like a Rainbow" to Mariah Green and Justin Perkins. The two of you are simply the best. Without your awesome collaborations this would not be a beautiful book. I believe nothing beats working side by side with amazing illustrators who understand how to make a book come alive. You both achieved the difficult task of nailing the illustrations, and getting this book across the finishing line.
I am forever grateful.

LaJuana Jackson

Just Like A Rainbow

Hey Shelby, what color are we?

You mean red, purple or blue we could be? Oh come on, tell me, what color are we?

We were created by God, you see. Just like the rainbow, God created you and me.

So maybe we are indigo? yellow? or green?

Ummm.... Well, God did make everything. Noooo, that's not it. Shelby, what color are we?

11

Caleb, we were created by God, you see.

12

Just like the rainbow,
God created you and me.

13

Maybe we're orange...

14

Yeah, orange –
that's what I'd like to be!

Caleb, we were created by God, you see. Just like the rainbow, God created you and me.

SO, WHAT COLOR ARE WE!

It's not about your color,
you see. Read your Bible.

18

Yes! Read your Bible, that's the key!

Well, the Bible doesn't talk about what is on the OUTside of me, it says what is most important is what is on the INside of me. Ohhh – I get it... I am created by God... I see!

21

I have God on the inside of me. The most important thing for me is to just love others – that's the key!

I am created by God –
I see!

23

Hey guys, guess what?
We are created by God,
you see.Just like the
rainbow, God created you
and me.

The meaning of this story

We are all created by God. We are all beautiful colors, just like the rainbow in the sky. But just like a rainbow, even though it is so beautiful, there is something way more important about a rainbow than just the beautiful colors.

Genesis 9:8–17
God put the rainbow in the sky to remind us
of His promise He made to all of us.

Matthew 22:37–40
Even though we are all created with beautiful and different skin colors on the outside, there is something much more important about us than just the color of our skin. God created us to love one another. We are to love God and love others. That's what's most important.

1 John 4:16
So, it doesn't matter what color you might be.
What matters is you were created by God to love, you see.
His love is what He put on the inside of you and me.

God's Promise To Us

Genesis 9:8-17 NLT

8 Then God told Noah and his sons,
9 "I hereby confirm my covenant with you and your descendants,
10 and with all the animals that were on the boat with you—the birds, the livestock, and all the wild animals—every living creature on earth.
11 Yes, I am confirming my covenant with you. Never again will floodwaters kill all living creatures; never again will a flood destroy the earth."
12 Then God said, "I am giving you a sign of my covenant with you and with all living creatures, for all generations to come.
13 I have placed my rainbow in the clouds. It is the sign of my covenant with you and with all the earth.
14 When I send clouds over the earth, the rainbow will appear in the clouds,
15 and I will remember my covenant with you and with all living creatures. Never again will the floodwaters destroy all life.
16 When I see the rainbow in the clouds, I will remember the eternal covenant between God and every living creature on earth."
17 Then God said to Noah, "Yes, this rainbow is the sign of the covenant I am confirming with all the creatures on earth."

Love One Another

Matthew 22:37-40 NKJV

37 Jesus said to him, "'You shall love the LORD your God with all your heart, with all your soul, and with all your mind.'
38 This is the first and great commandment.
39 And the second is like it: 'You shall love your neighbor as yourself.'
40 On these two commandments hang all the Law and the Prophets."

Just Like A Rainbow Too

Hi Friend, – it's me, Caleb! Let's have some fun with colors

RED

ORANGE

YELLOW

GREEN

BLUE

INDIGO

VIOLET

BROWN

BLACK

WHITE

This is the color RED. Can you name all of the RED pictures on this page?

heart

fire truck

RED

crayon

HIDDEN PICTURES

Now can you find those RED objects in this picture?

This is the color ORANGE. Can you name all of the ORANGE pictures on this page?

Carrot

ORANGE

Basketball

Crayon

HIDDEN PICTURES
Now can you find those ORANGE objects in this picture?

This is the color YELLOW. Can you name all of the YELLOW pictures on this page?

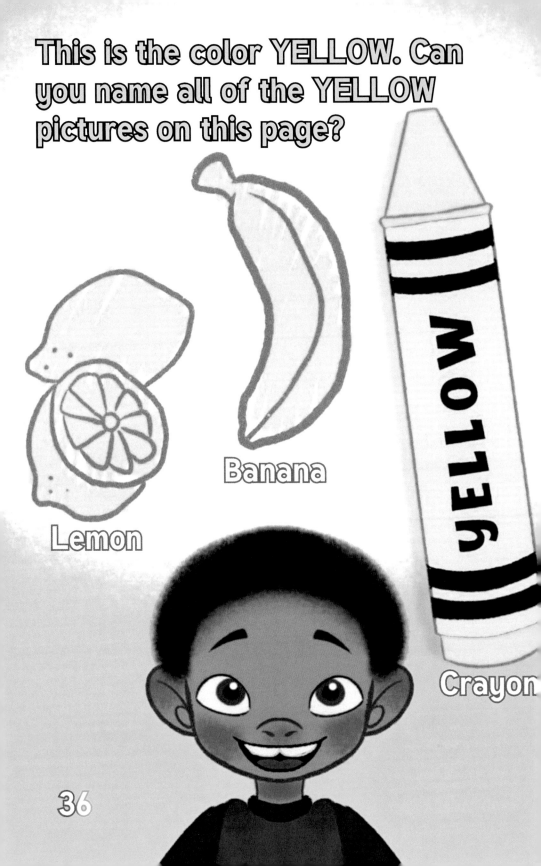

Banana

Lemon

YELLOW

Crayon

HIDDEN PICTURES
Now can you find those YELLOW objects in this picture?

This is the color BLUE. Can you name all of the BLUE pictures on this page?

Cap

Bird

Crayon

HIDDEN PICTURES
Now can you find those BLUE objects in this picture?

This is the color INDIGO. Can you name all of the INDIGO pictures on this page?

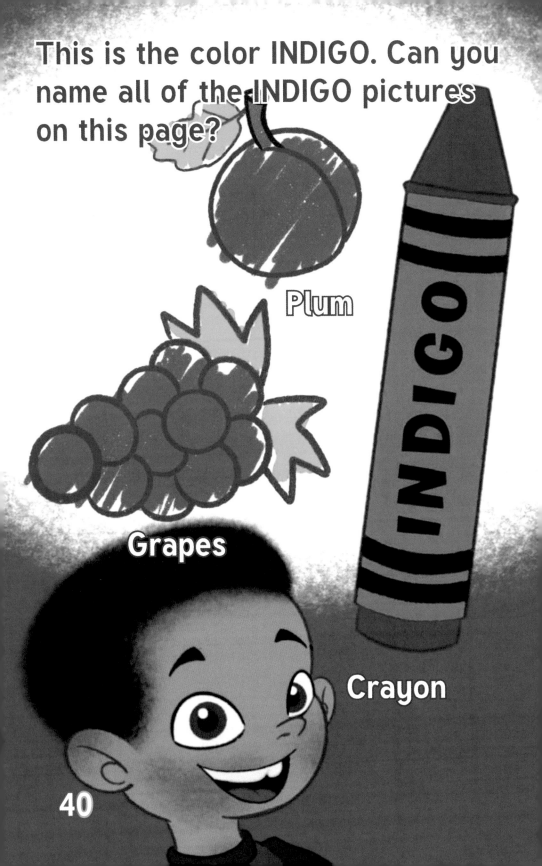

Plum

Grapes

INDIGO

Crayon

HIDDEN PICTURES
Now can you find those INDIGO objects in this picture?

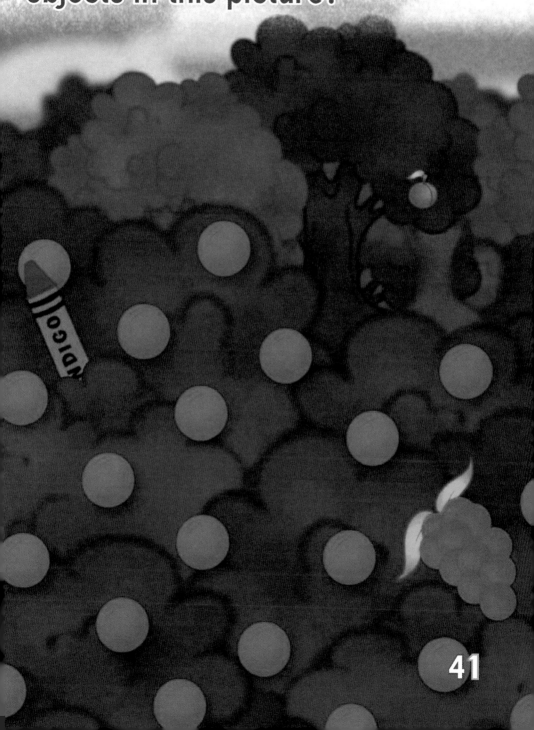

41

This is the color GREEN. Can you name all of the GREEN pictures on this page?

Apple

Frog

GREEN

Crayon

HIDDEN PICTURES
Now can you find those GREEN objects in this picture?

43

This is the color BLACK. Can you name all of the BLACK pictures on this page?

Crayon

Crow

Glasses

HIDDEN PICTURES
Now can you find those BLACK objects in this picture?

This is the color BROWN. Can you name all of the BROWN pictures on this page?

Acorn

Squirrel

BROWN

Crayon

HIDDEN PICTURES
Now can you find those BROWN objects in this picture?

47

This is the color VIOLET. Can you name all of the VIOLET pictures on this page?

Balloon

Flower

Crayon

VIOLET

HIDDEN PICTURES
Now can you find those VIOLET objects in this picture?

49

This is the color WHITE. Can you name all of the WHITE pictures on this page?

Mouse

Bunny

WHITE

Crayon

HIDDEN PICTURES
Now can you find those WHITE objects in this picture?

51

Can you find these hidden pictures?

Thanks Friend,
For having some fun with colors.

Remember, it doesn't matter what color you are. You are beautiful and special just like a rainbow. God loves us all.

Available now on Amazon,
From  Power of One

poweroflegucates.com

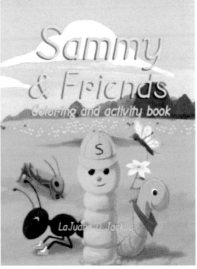

56